I GROW ON YOU

SOUMYA RAHA

Made with ♥ on the Notion Press Platform
www.notionpress.com

Dedicated to my Mom and Dad,

Love you both.

Contents

Preface

Most of the writings are the thoughts penned down out of sheer imagination

and unrelatable to any true happenings.

The poems promise to touch the readers in each of their own ways.

The perspectives of all of them may or may not be the ones happening around us.

The barriers are broken keeping in mind the trust and the sensitivity of the readers all over.

Some may sound cruel enough though they represent the sole purpose to inflict in each of them with an honest opinion and ownership.

Dedicated to all the readers,

My love is with you all.

Acknowledgements

This is written in a format of poetry exploring erotica & thrill. This format is widely used globally. I am inspired by many books that follow the similar template where poetry is not limited to a specific pattern but is narrative. Each poetry uncovers a story. Hope you all like what you read here...

1. Never Stop Being So Dominant

I heard you already
You haven't said a word.
Is it a game or a trick?
To know me or eat me out
I don't fear you.
I never wanted a reason
You kept on growing on me
Slowly till I sleep
I feel you inside
My lips, my thighs, my curves
You grew everywhere.
Are you so dominating?
Are you literally damaged?
I fear the damage done to you once
I promise I won't ever harm
The reason is I love you so madly
Our madness even heals my wounds.

2. Would you kiss me again?

Hey! My Hotness! I need you now
Would you kiss me again?
Yes I stabbed you thrice
One for the pain
Second for the gain
Third to avenge
I licked you all over
Even after remembering
What you've done to me
You won't remember
You forget soon
The game of yours
I was too immature to know
I saw things break, people cry
The Nightmares! Oh, my lady
This blood marks the end of you & me
Keep your eyes open to see me die too
For I haven't slept with you in pain, but in Love.

3. I miss your smell

You never visit me now
It feels so lonely
We dreamt of being together forever
It pains to stay without you.
You rarely visit me now
You never hug me tight now
You talk less, cry more
I don't even know why
I sleep without you each day
Would you not tell me the reason?
The real reason behind those tears.
I still miss your breath
I miss your smell
My pillow knows me so well
It hides your panties underneath
I even kept it hidden from the monsters here
They drug me and force me to sleep
I don't wanna spend the rest of my life
It feels like I am in an Asylum.

4. Who touches you now?

I die each day to know someone else
Touches you always
He fucks you madly
I feel like cutting his body in hundred parts
To feed the hungry dogs
I will slit his throat to undo what's done
Break his head
The dirty head thinks of you
Fantasizes you
Touches you all over that body
He explores each places I visited
He kills me each time he eats you
Each slap on your tits pains me
He uses you again and again
You are dumb fucking ass to not understand me
He is a moron to rule over you
You could have led a Queen's life
But you chose to be a bitch instead.

5. Being lonely is so addictive

Just wondering the days passed

Things changed so quickly

You can't keep the moments frozen for you

Change is inevitable

It's just you start learning

That things will be unplanned

May be a mess sometimes

You try hard to keep

But things will fall apart

You might be afraid of not showing up the best of you

But you start staying alone

You seem to enjoy the tranquility that lies within

You enjoy classics, cut the rope loose

You start walking alone

You see none to disappoint

Keeping your head high you face the storms

Leaving all addictions you crave to be alone again

You quickly start healing again

Each day triggers a new tomorrow

Feel strong again

Because you are learning to stay alone again.

6. Remember the kiss

Remember the day we kissed
It was raining heavily outside
The mountains, dark and beautiful like those monsters
The clouds covering the naked sky
We kept on kissing
Lost in thoughts
Feeling each other's breathe
You looked bright
You hugged me tight
Pulled me closest as if a promise
Never to let me go
My hands cherishing your hair
Playing with your skin
We were so lost in each other
That we stepped out in the rain
Danced in the rain, like never before
Felt like living the best day
Remember the day we kissed
It was magical.

7. We both are explorers

I visit your body each day
Each time you grab me in
It feels new always
Exploring the places
The desires to fulfill
The satisfaction to honor
Your body is like the purest temple
The lips, the cheeks, the breath
The cleavage that smells
Seductive enough to lose my breath
You love me inside you every time
Even from top & behind
Each time you moan, you moan loud
You love me when I lose my control
You crave to ride me till you sweat more
The shape I dismantle, rub and pushes
You blow me well like some classic tune played each time
You swallow me enough each time
We are the travellers who lost their way
In the mid of the sea
The waves, aura of erotica makes us vulnerable
We fight, we challenge, we lose

We flow the way two magnets attract
You pull me to explore the holes
We both unleash the wildest beast from within
We are both travellers & explorers
Exploring each other daily.

8. I wait for the call

I call you twice daily
To know you more
We felt it's necessary
To learn about each other
Before the day
Aah! I can't wait to see
You dressed as a bride
Those eyes shining bright
Cute cheeks glowing
It seems I am in a rush
To accept the responsibility
In a rush to cuddle you after a hectic day
In a rush to sleep on your lap and feel at home
In a rush to stay with you forever till death sets us apart
Said this before, I say it again
You keep me alive
I live for you
I love you my love
Love you always
Love you forever

9. Is this a Goodbye?

Babe, you are cold today

I stand still

Why don't you hug me again?

Is this a goodbye?

What did you go through?

I won't let you live in that box

Please let me sleep beside you again

For we both have ended

The Touch I look forward to each day

Madness, to crave again

Redundant yet mind blown each time

Those hills to live in

The shape to die for

The smell to get addicted

The messy hair which rests on my fingers

Till we lose our breath

Could I ever imagine you with someone else?

The guilty craves in

For we both are committed

We both are guilty

Guilty to break a promise

The promise to die together

I can't let you go
Never ever I can, I won't
Wait for me I am coming
As I said we both ended.

10. The Chapter of Betrayal

He pulls the trigger
Moments froze
Memories stolen
Fear of being alone again
Pretending to be calm
Struggling to forget
Struggling to forgive
He won't let her live anymore
He would kill again if she cheats
He would kill the fear, the trauma
This moonlit night must mark the end
Chapter must end
The Chapter of Betrayal.

The End

Did the Book grow on you?

Don't worry, it will...